Book 1

Ick and Crud

Ick's Bleh Day

by Wiley Blevins • illustrated by Jim Paillot

RED
CHAIR
•PRESS•

D1165195

Funny Bone Books

and Funny Bone Readers are produced and published by

Red Chair Press LLC   PO Box 333   South Egremont, MA 01258-0333

www.redchairpress.com

About the Author

Wiley Blevins has taught elementary school in both the United States and South America. He has also written over 60 books for children and 15 for teachers, as well as created reading programs for schools in the U.S. and Asia with Scholastic, Macmillan/McGraw-Hill, Houghton-Mifflin Harcourt, and other publishers. Wiley currently lives and writes in New York City.

About the Artist

Jim Paillot is a dad, husband and illustrator. He lives in Arizona with his family and two dogs and any other animal that wants to come in out of the hot sun. When not illustrating, Jim likes to hike, watch cartoons and collect robots.

Publisher's Cataloging-In-Publication Data

Names: Blevins, Wiley. | Paillot, Jim, illustrator.

Title: Ick and Crud. Book 1, Ick's bleh day / by Wiley Blevins ; illustrated by Jim Paillot.

Other Titles: Ick's bleh day

Description: South Egremont, MA : Red Chair Press, [2017] | Series: First chapters | Interest age level: 005-007. | Summary: "Ick is feeling down, under-the-weather BLEH! But lucky for him, his pal Crud is there to cheer him up."--Provided by publisher.

Identifiers: LCCN 2016947293 | ISBN 978-1-63440-185-2 (library hardcover) | ISBN 978-1-63440-188-3 (paperback) | ISBN 978-1-63440-191-3 (ebook)

Subjects: LCSH: Friendship--Juvenile fiction. | Sick--Juvenile fiction. | Dogs--Juvenile fiction. | CYAC: Friendship--Fiction. | Sick--Fiction. | Dogs--Fiction.

Classification: LCC PZ7.B618652 Ici 2017 (print) | LCC PZ7.B618652 (ebook) | DDC [E]--dc23

Printed in the United States of America

0517 1P CGBF17

Table of Contents

Meet the Characters

Crud

Ick

Miss Puffy

Bob

Fun in the Mud

"**W**hat's wrong, Ick?" asked Crud.

"I'm feeling *bleh*," said Ick.

"*Bleh?*" asked Crud.

"Yes," said Ick. "Sad. Bad. Bored."

"Oh," said Crud. "Then we need to fix that. You need to feel good like me, buddy."

"Hmmm," thought Ick. "It *would* be great to feel like Crud."

"Let me think of a way to cheer you up," said Crud. "Would you like a dog bone?"

"No," said Ick. "I would not like a dog bone."

"Would you like to chase a squirrel?" asked Crud.

"No," said Ick. "I would not like to chase a squirrel."

"Would you like to see me dance?" asked Crud.

"No," said Ick. "I would not like to see you dance. No one would."

"Then what about some ice cream?" asked Crud.

Ick sat up. "I think I would like that," he said.

"Then let's get some," said Crud.

Ick and Crud set off for the one place that always had ice cream. The park.

They raced through their yard, jumped over the fence, and landed in Mrs. Martin's yard. *Splat!* Mud flew everywhere.

"This is not ice cream," said Ick.
"But it is gooey and fun."

"Do you feel less *bleh* now?" asked Crud.

Ick shook his head. "Only a little."

"Then let's keep going," said Crud.

Just then something moved above them.
The two froze.

"I will if you will," whispered Ick.

Ick and Crud slowly looked up. Miss Puffy sat on the fence. Her tail flipped from side to side. She licked her paws like they were lollipops.

"You two are *dis-gust-ing*," she purred.

"We're what?" asked Ick.

"*Dis... gust...* oh, never mind," said Miss Puffy. "How will you two ever get clean? Like me."

"Maybe it will rain again," said Ick.

Crud looked up at the now clear blue sky. "Or maybe not," he said.

Miss Puffy lifted her head. The light bounced off something on her neck.

"What's that?" asked Ick.

"You're blinding us," said Crud.

"It's my new collar," said Miss Puffy. "*Real* diamonds." She stood and strutted up and down the fence. "My owner bought it in Paris. Do you like?"

Crud rolled his eyes.

"Bob bought our collars closer to home," said Ick.

"Bob made our collars," whispered Crud.

Miss Puffy laughed. Then she shook her head so her diamond collar sparkled in the light.

"Hey Ick," whispered Crud. "Wanna have even more fun?"

"Yes!" said Ick.

"Then shake," said Crud.

"Shake?" asked Ick.

"Yes," said Crud. "Shake like an earthquake."

So Ick shook. And off flew the mud.

Fling! Sling! Splash! Miss Puffy hissed and dashed away.

"Sorry," yelled Ick.

"Sort of," whispered Crud.

"Do you feel less *bleh* now?" asked Crud.

Ick shook his head. "Only a little."

"Wait until we get to the park," said Crud.

Glub, Glub, Glub

Ick and Crud skipped down the street, around the corner, and past the big trash cans. They stopped to sniff the cans, the trash around the cans, and then each other. *Sniff. Sniff. What a whiff!*

When they were finished sniffing, they ran down another street, around another corner, and into the park. They both skidded to a stop. Crud looked all around. "Where is it?" he asked.

"Where is what?" asked Ick.

"The big pink truck," said Crud. "With all the ice cream."

"It's not here," said Ick. "What do we do now? I still feel *bleh.*"

Crud stopped to think, which is easier to do when you have ice cream in your belly.

"I've got it!" said Crud. "Would you like to play *Bob*?"

"Okay," said Ick. "It's fun to play *Bob*. How do you play *Bob* again?"

"I give an order," said Crud. "And you do what I say."

"That is fun!" said Ick.

"Okay," said Crud. He put a stick in his mouth and tossed it away. "Fetch!" yelled Crud. Ick ran after the stick. He ran into the tall grasses until...

...a butterfly flapped above him. He stopped to look at its black and orange wings. "You're so pretty," Ick said. Then he rolled on his back and watched the butterfly dip down and land on his nose. "So pretty," said Ick again.

"Hey Ick," yelled Crud. "Did you get the stick?"

"Stick?" asked Ick. He sat up.

"Yes. The stick I threw," said Crud.

"Oh, that stick," said Ick. "Where is it?" Crud pointed. Ick crawled through the grass and looked all around.

Here a stick. There a stick. Everywhere a stick-stick. But not *his* stick. "Never mind," said Crud.

Ick ran back to Crud. "Let's try again," Ick said.

"Okay," said Crud. "Roll over and bark."

"You sound just like Bob," said Ick.

"So do it," said Crud.

Ick did. He rolled to the right. Then he rolled to the left. He rolled and rolled and rolled until...

...he rolled right down the hill. And he rolled and rolled and rolled until he stopped at the edge of a small pond.

Croak... croak... croak. "What was that?" asked Ick. Crud ran to him. *Croak... croak... ribbit.*

Two eyes popped out of the water. "A monster!" yelled Ick. Ick jumped on Crud's back.

"Get off," said Crud. Crud swayed back and forth, and forth and back, and side to side, and up and down.

SPLAT! The two fell into the pond. *Glub... glub... glub.* Ick popped out of the water.

Croak. A frog jumped off his head. "Goodbye, frog," said Ick. "You're so pretty. And nothing like a monster."

Then Crud popped out of the water.
Ribbit. A frog sat on his face. He peeled
it off.

"Well at least we're clean now," said Ick.

"And?" asked Crud. "Do you feel
less *bleh*?"

Ick shook his head. "Only a little."

Crud sighed. But then he heard a noise.
The noise he had been waiting for.

"Do you hear that ding-dong-ding-a-gong?" asked Crud.

"Yes," said Ick. "What is it?"

"It's the ice cream truck's bell," said Crud. "Run!" The two raced up the hill, through the tall grasses, and to the side of the big pink truck.

A tall, thin man handed out ice cream cones. Big ones. Little ones. And ones with sprinkles. But he didn't give Ick and Crud one. He didn't even seem to see them.

"What do we do now?" asked Ick

"Stand next to a kid," whispered Crud. "The smaller, the better."

"Why?" asked Ick.

"They are the first to drop their cones," said Crud

"Then what?" asked Ick.

"Then you lick like your tongue is on fire."

"Got it," said Ick. "My tongue is ready."

Ick scooted over to a short-short kid.
Ick looked up. The little boy licked at
his cone. "Yum," thought Ick.

"Double yum," thought Crud and
he barked louder than he meant to.
The frightened kid dropped his cone.
"WAAAAAHHHHHHH!!!"

"Get it," yelled Crud.

Ick dove for the cone, his tongue ready
for the lick-lick-licking.

"WAAAAAAHHHHHHHH!!!" Ick grabbed
the cone in his mouth and looked up at
the little boy. "Oh, no," thought Ick.
"He feels more *bleh* than me now."

So instead of woofing down the cone, Ick handed it to the boy. The kid grabbed the cone and went back to licking.

The tall, thin man poked his head out of the truck to see what all the crying was about. He spotted Ick and Crud. "Scram!" he yelled.

"Run!" said Crud.

The two raced around the big pink truck, behind the long park benches, along the bike path, and onto the sidewalk. They skidded to a stop.

"Sorry about the ice cream," said Crud.

"Not me," said Ick.

"No?" asked Crud.

"No," said Ick. "I no longer feel *bleh*. Now I feel like Ick."

"Like *ick*?" asked Crud.

"Yes," said Ick. "I feel like myself again."

"Great," said Crud. "Then let's go home, buddy."

And off they went, sniff, sniff,
sniffing all the way home.